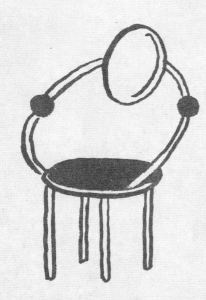

MICHELE DE LUCCHI
Italy
First Chair 1983

FRANK LLOYD WRIGHT
United States
Fallingwater 1935

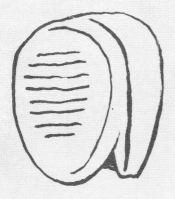

ISAMU NOGUCHI
United States
Radio Nurse 1937

JORGE FERRARI-HARDOY
Argentina
Hardoy Chair 1938

ALDO ROSSI
Italy
La Conica Espresso Pot 1984

PHILIPPE STARCK
France
Voxan GTV 1200 2008

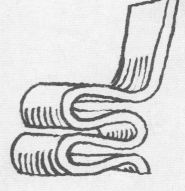

FRANK GEHRY
United States
Wiggle Side Chair 1972

To Nora

I'd like to thank Marzia and Maurizio, and everyone at Corraini
Editore, for their patience, and for providing the best studio
an illustrator could hope for.
I'd like to thank all of the architects and designers who
inspired the illustrations in this book.
And I'd like to thank Nora, for everything, but especially
for letting me drag her to Mantova for five weeks, where this
book finally came into focus.

Cataloging-in-Publication Data has been applied for and may be obtained from the Library of Congress.

ISBN 978-0-8109-8941-2

First Italian edition published by Maurizio Corraini srl in 2009

Printed and bound in Italy

10 9 8

ABRAMS The Art of Books
195 Broadway, New York, NY 10007
abramsbooks.com

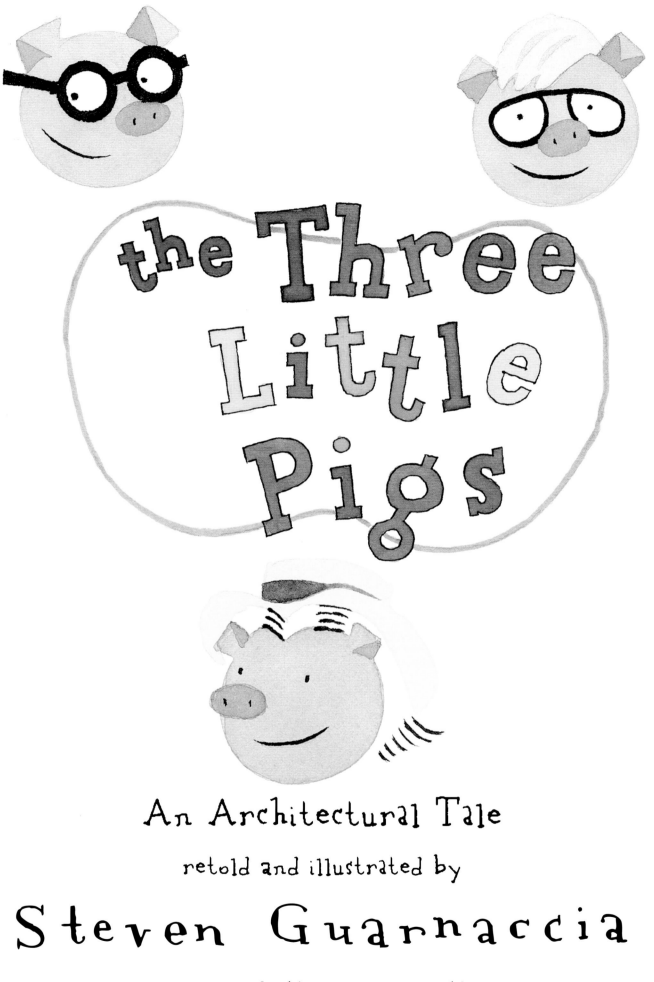

the Three Little Pigs

An Architectural Tale

retold and illustrated by

Steven Guarnaccia

Abrams Books for Young Readers, New York

Once upon a time, there were three little pigs who lived in a big house in the forest. One day the three pigs said good-bye to their mother and went off to make their way in the world.

The first little pig decided to build his house of scraps.

The second little pig decided to build his house of glass.

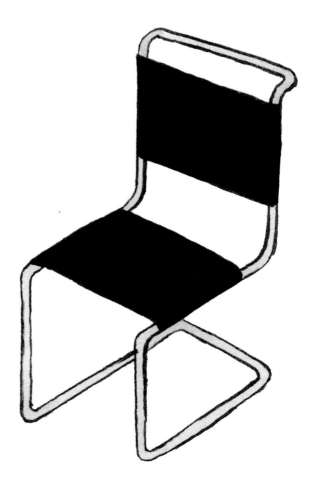

But the third little
pig decided to build
his house of stone
and concrete.

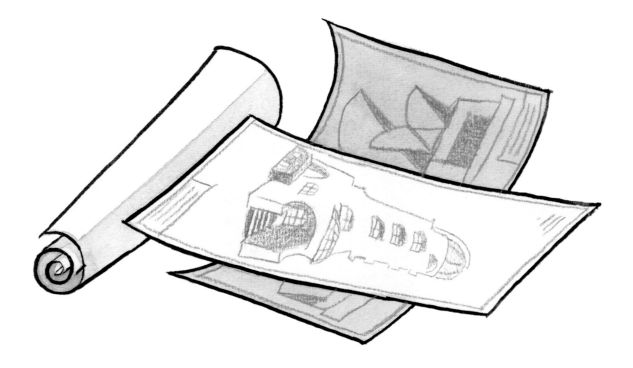

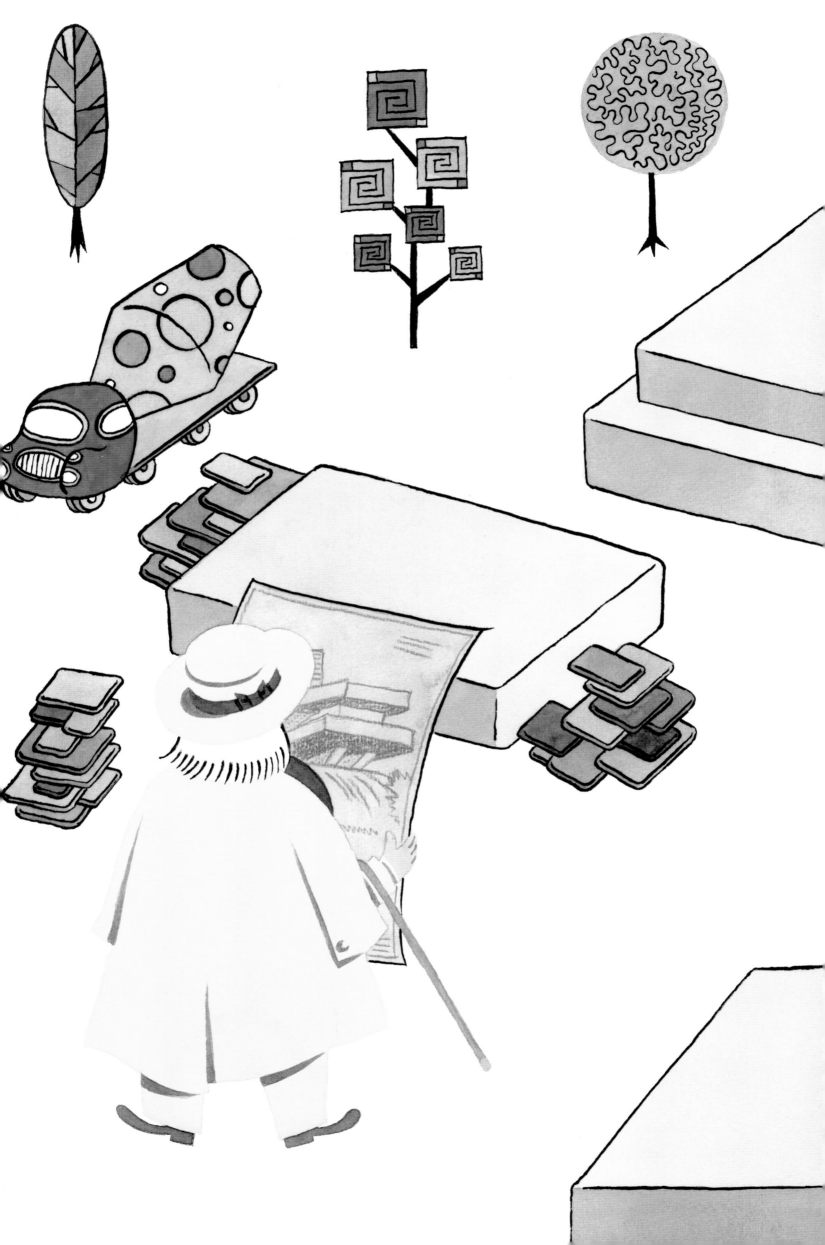

Now, there was an evil wolf who lived in the woods nearby. One day he came to the house of the first little pig and said, "Little pig, little pig, let me come in." But the pig answered, "Not by the hair of my chinny-chin-chin."

This made the wolf so angry that
he said, "Then I'll huff, and I'll puff, and
I'll blow YOUR house in." The wolf huffed,
and he puffed, and he blew the house of
scraps away.

The first little pig ran as fast as he could to
the house of his brother.

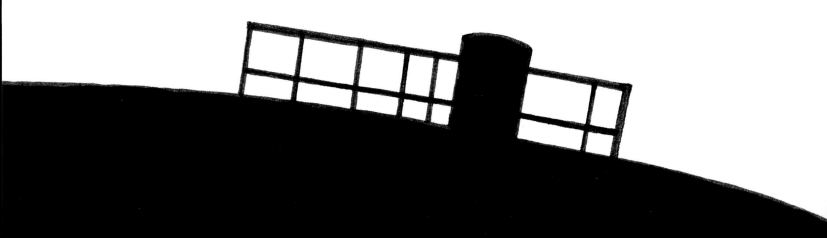

Soon the wolf came to the house of the second little pig. The wolf called out, "Little pig, little pig, let me come in."

The second pig answered, "Not by the hair of my chinny-chin-chin." The wolf gnashed his teeth and said, "Then I'll huff, and I'll puff, and I'll blow YOUR house in."

And the wolf huffed, and he puffed, and he blew the house of glass to smithereens.

So the two little pigs ran as fast as their legs would take them to the house of their brother.

Finally, the wolf arrived at the house of the third little pig. The wolf growled at the door, "Little pig, little pig, let me come in."

But the third little pig replied, "Not by the hair of my chinny-chin-chin."

This enraged the evil wolf, who roared, "Then I'll huff, and I'll puff, and I'll blow YOUR house in."

So he huffed, and he puffed, and he puffed, and he huffed, but he couldn't budge the house of stone and concrete.

The wolf said, "Little pig, meet me tomorrow morning at 7:00 at Farmer Wright's, and I'll show you a fine tomato greenhouse."

But the pig awoke at 6:00,
picked the best tomatoes in the
greenhouse, and was home
slicing them for lunch by the time
the wolf arrived.

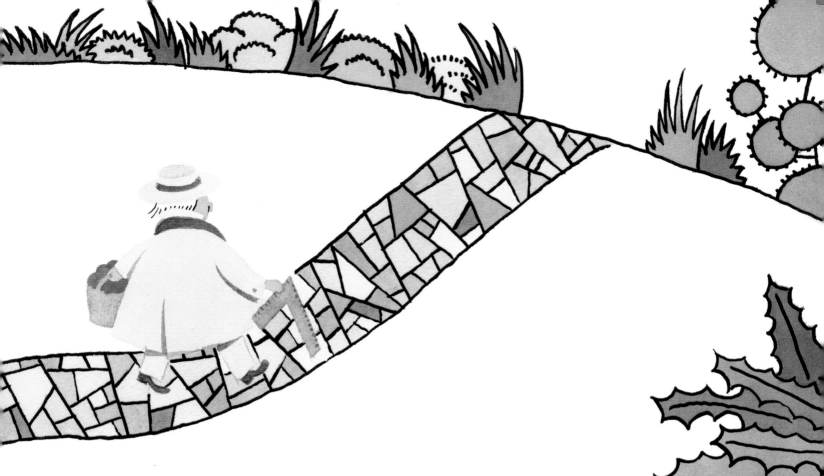

"I'll get you yet!" said the
wolf under his breath.

The wolf returned to the third pig's house and said, "Little pig, meet me tomorrow morning at 6:00 at Farmer Johnson's, and I'll show you an orchard full of tasty apples."

The next morning at 5:00, the pig was picking the best apples in Farmer Johnson's orchard when along came the wolf. "Good, aren't they?" said the wolf. "They certainly are!" said the pig. "Here, try one!" As the wolf chased the apple, the third pig ran home to his house of stone and concrete.

That evening the wolf went back to the third little pig's house and said, "I'll meet you at Frank's Flea Market tomorrow morning at 5:00." So the pig arrived at 4:00. He was admiring a fine rug when he saw the wolf approaching.

He hid himself in the rug and rolled down the hill toward the wolf. The wolf sped away, with the rug following after him. The third pig returned home, where he and his brothers prepared a roaring fire in the fireplace and settled in for the evening.

Tricked again, the wolf rushed to the third pig's house, saying under his breath, "Little pigs, I'll get you yet!"

The wolf climbed onto the roof and shouted down the chimney, "I'm coming in to get you!" But the wolf tumbled into the roaring fire, scorching his tail.

The wolf ran from the house, smoke streaming after him, and was never seen in the forest again.

The three little pigs ate a supper of tomato soup and apple pie, and they lived happily ever after.

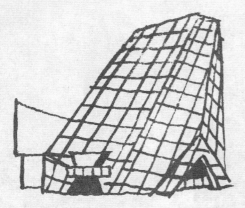

COOP HIMMELB(L)AU
Austria
UFA Cinema Center 1998

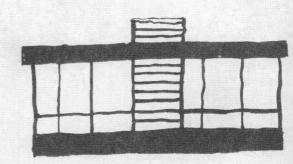

PHILIP JOHNSON
United States
The Glass House 1949

FRANK GEHRY
United States
Gehry House 1978

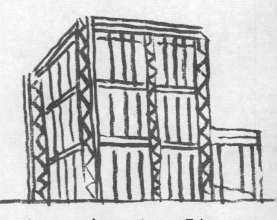

GEORGE FRED KECK
United States
The Crystal House 1934

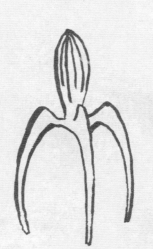

PHILIPPE STARCK
France
Juicy Salif Juicer 1990

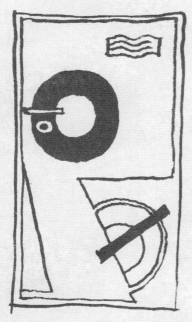

EILEEN GRAY
Ireland
Marine D'Abord Rug 1927

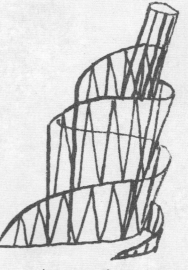

VLADIMIR TATLIN
Russia
Monument for
The Third International 1920